David Paul Brown

Eulogium on the Life and Character of the Late Honourable

Joseph Reed Ingersoll

David Paul Brown

Eulogium on the Life and Character of the Late Honourable Joseph Reed Ingersoll

ISBN/EAN: 9783337425067

Printed in Europe, USA, Canada, Australia, Japan

Cover: Foto ©Raphael Reischuk / pixelio.de

More available books at **www.hansebooks.com**

EULOGIUM

ON THE

LIFE AND CHARACTER

OF THE LATE

HON. JOSEPH REED INGERSOLL,

PRESIDENT OF THE HISTORICAL SOCIETY OF PENNSYLVANIA.

BY

DAVID PAUL BROWN.

Delivered Sept. 28, 1869.

AT THE HALL OF THE UNIVERSITY OF PENNSYLVANIA.

Published in Pursuance of a Resolution of the Society.

PHILADELPHIA:
COLLINS, PRINTER, 705 JAYNE STREET.
1869.

NOTE.

The Historical Society of Pennsylvania, desirous to honor the memory of its late President, Hon. JOSEPH REED INGERSOLL, adopted a resolution inviting David Paul Brown, Esq., to deliver an address commemorative of his life and character.

Mr. BROWN, having accepted the duty to which he was thus invited, delivered the following Eulogium in the Hall of the University of Pennsylvania, on the evening of the 28th of September, 1869.

The Hall was filled with a large audience, composed of eminent citizens of Philadelphia.

CORRESPONDENCE.

THE HISTORICAL SOCIETY OF PENNSYLVANIA,
PHILADELPHIA, March 24, 1869.

MY DEAR SIR,

At a meeting of the Executive Council of the Historical Society of Pennsylvania, held on the 22d inst., a resolution was adopted inviting you to deliver before the Society, a eulogium upon the life and character of our late President, Hon. Joseph R. Ingersoll.

In communicating this resolution to you, I express the earnest hope and desire of the Society that it may suit your views and convenience to comply with this request.

The time for its delivery is left entirely to your option and convenience.

With the highest respect,

I have the honor to be

Your friend and obedient servant,

JAMES ROSS SNOWDEN,
Chairman Executive Council.

DAVID PAUL BROWN, ESQ., Philadelphia.

No. 1113 GIRARD STREET,
PHILADELPHIA, March 26, 1869.

To JAMES ROSS SNOWDEN, ESQ.,
Corresponding Secretary of Historical Society of Pennsylvania.

MY DEAR SIR,

I have received your letter in behalf of the Historical Society announcing my appointment to deliver a eulogy upon the life and character of the Honorable Joseph Reed Ingersoll, the late President of the Society, and also expressing a hope that I might comply with their request. In answer to this invitation, allow me to say, that I can refuse nothing that is intended to do honor to the memory of my departed and lamented FRIEND, and that the only hesitation I feel in assuming this grateful task, arises from the consciousness of my inadequacy to do justice to the exalted merits of the subject. Diffidence, however, upon such an occasion, must give place to sympathetic duty, and I therefore not only willingly, but gratefully accept the appointment.

With great regard,

Very truly yours,

DAVID PAUL BROWN.

HISTORICAL SOCIETY OF PENNSYLVANIA.
PHILADELPHIA, October 6, 1869.

To DAVID PAUL BROWN, Esq.

MY DEAR SIR,

The Historical Society of Pennsylvania, and the large and intelligent audience present, listened with the liveliest satisfaction and gratification to your eloquent eulogium on the life and character of Mr. Ingersoll.

At the close of the exercises, the resolutions were adopted which I have the honor herewith to send you, and in doing so I beg to express the hope that you will comply with the request therein presented.

The publication of such an address is, in many respects, greatly to be desired ; more especially as examples of lives and characters, such as was exhibited in the career of our late President, so happily and appropriately delineated by you, are proper studies for the imitations of our people, and for the elevation of the moral and intellectual condition of our country.

I am, dear sir, with the highest respect,

Your friend and obedient servant,

JAMES ROSS SNOWDEN,
Corresponding Secretary His. So. of Penna.

———

PHILADELPHIA, October 6, 1869.

To HON. JAMES ROSS SNOWDEN,

Corresponding Secretary of the Historical Society of Pennsylvania.

DEAR SIR,

I have just received your kind letter in behalf of the Historical Society of Pennsylvania, requesting a copy of the eulogy pronounced by me upon the life and character of the Hon. Joseph Reed Ingersoll, the late President of the Society, and my *life-long* friend. The eulogy is entirely at your service, accompanied, however, with the sincere regret that it is not more worthy of the subject, and of the distinguished audience before which it was delivered.

Accept my thanks for the Society, and for yourself my lasting and affectionate regard.

DAVID PAUL BROWN.

INTRODUCTORY REMARKS.

BY

JOHN WILLIAM WALLACE, ESQ.,

PRESIDENT OF THE HISTORICAL SOCIETY.

LADIES AND GENTLEMEN :—

WE are assembled this evening in pursuance of an invitation from the Historical Society of Pennsylvania. As there must be many persons in this large assembly who are not members of that association, I may take leave, perhaps, to state that the Society was founded in the year 1824, and that its object is the collection, preservation, arrangement, and publication of such historical things as contribute to the truth of history and add to the dignity and honor of our city, State and nation. Although the corporation has never been in any way publicly endowed, it has now existed for nearly half a century, and has become, in fact, a stable institution of the State. Indeed, it has so increased, of late, in capacities of usefulness, that it not long since issued a circular giving to its members information of some particulars of its condition. From this, corrected up to the present day,

we learn that it has a library of historical works,
numbering about 17,000 books, and of pamphlets full
80,000. In the department of pamphlets, indeed,
which embraces the invaluable collection recently
bequeathed to us by our fellow-member, Mr. G. W.
Fahnestock, the Society is singularly rich. It pos-
sesses also a considerable museum, constantly aug-
menting by gifts, in which are preserved many
curious relics of Washington, Penn, and others, illustrious in our civic and social annals; and a gallery
of portraits embracing many of our revolutionary
officers, and of our early governors and statesmen
and men of letters. We have a fund now amounting
to $16,000 for the publication of manuscripts, and by
means of this four large and elegant volumes have
been already printed. The president here exhibited
one of these handsome works, remarking upon the
interesting value of its contents. The publication of
another is now completed. We have, too, a building
fund now amounting to $12,000, and which interest
and contributions are increasing. It is the hope of
the Society before many years to be able to erect an
edifice worthy of the city in which its treasures may
be conveniently arranged and properly exhibited, and
where they may be beyond the ordinary risks of fire.
In the mean time, its hall is in the upper floor of the
Athenaeum Building in Sixth Street. Should any of
you, not members of the Society, feel disposed to visit
it, in behalf of the body I cordially invite you to do so.
Our worthy and courteous librarian, the Rev. Dr.

Shrigley, will be happy, I am sure, to welcome any of you and to show to you whatever among our treasures it may most interest you to see.

To proceed to the more immediate subject which engages us this evening :—

The Society is assembled to-night, and has done itself the honor to invite hither those of you who are not of its members, in order to commemorate the virtues and services of its late President, the Honorable JOSEPH REED INGERSOLL, a gentleman who, born on this soil, and living for more than eighty years among this people, touched this community at so many points —professionally as a much admired advocate at our bar—politically, as a representative from this city in Congress, and afterwards as the representative of the nation abroad—in the religious aspect, as a frequent participant in the councils of the church of which he was a member—and socially, and in civic relations, as a hospitable and liberally minded gentleman, open and of access easy to all—that there can be but few present, I should suppose, if of mature years at all, who had not some acquaintance with him, either through the pleasure of personal intercourse, or by his good fame and his good deeds ; and none who, having known him, will not readily understand why the Historical Society, of which he was long the President and benefactor, should now, on his death, desire to pay to his memory a mark of its respect.

Scarcely less known in this community than was Mr. Ingersoll himself is the gentleman to whom we shall be indebted for a discourse commemorative of him. I feel that on this occasion, I need not introduce the orator. For when before my fellow-citizens of Philadelphia, I pronounce the name of DAVID PAUL BROWN, I pronounce a name as familiar to the most of them as that of the honored city in which they live.

Mr. Brown now came forward and delivered a eulogy, as follows:—

EULOGY.

It is a great honor—if, while our thoughts are resting upon the grave, we may be permitted to speak of *worldly* honors—it is indeed a great honor, thus to be invited, or even allowed, to address so large, so learned, so distinguished, and so brilliant an assemblage, upon this mournful, though grateful occasion. But while entering upon my duty in regard to these sad designs, I trust with becoming diffidence, I have still no apologies to make. I should be ashamed to mingle deliberate, premeditated, and cold-blooded excuses, with a tribute to the cherished memory of a lamented and departed FRIEND. This is a duty of Love, and duties assumed are duties to be discharged. If the task be faithfully performed apologies are unnecessary; if, unhappily, it should fail, they would serve only to increase the delinquency. I therefore proceed at once to the humble fulfilment of my allotted task; a task not only impressive to myself, but impressive to the entire community, who sympathize, and suffer in that bereavement, which we must all naturally and deeply deplore, in the loss of an aged and most distinguished fellow-citizen, an accomplished scholar, a public benefactor, and above all, and embracing all, an exemplary and devout Christian. If *affection* could supply the ability for such a theme, I might hope to transfuse into your hearts the sorrows of my own. But, alas! it too often happens that the depth of our emotions impairs their adequate expression. *Language* is too weak and cold to portray, truly, the emotions of the *soul*. These can be only felt, and known, in the communion of the heart with itself. Still, that which is impossible may at least be honestly attempted, and the failure even pardoned, from the merit and sincerity of the motive.

The memorials and examples of illustrious men, who, after a long life of labor and deserved distinction, have in the fulness of time, like the sun showing their greatest countenance in their lowest estate, sunk into the grave, life's dark and inevitable horizon, are always appropriate and salutary lessons to those who shall survive. And there is, therefore, a peculiar propriety in this duty being assumed upon the present occasion by the Historical Society of Pennsylvania.

Mr. Ingersoll was the *President* of this Institution, a native of the State, and an honor to the State. His name well deserves to be historical. He was the Cicero of the American Bar, and he may be truly said to be one of Plutarch's men, nay, if I have read his annals rightly, one of the noblest of them.

To commemorate *such* a man is not so essential to the preservation of *his fame*, as to that of those who have enjoyed the benefit of his magnanimous example; and in whom a want of desert might be fairly inferred, from an omission to express their gratitude upon an occasion so peculiarly appropriate as the present.

It is not to reward *him*, for if private and public worth be an earnest of future bliss, he has already received an *unearthly* reward in the bosom of his Saviour. But it is to inculcate upon *others* the moral beauty and value of his example, that we my fellow-citizens, are now assembled.

The feelings and principles manifested by his arduous public and professional career, while they show how little remained to him for the enjoyment of social and domestic peace, bear unequivocal evidence of a head and heart replete with every moral and intellectual refinement and excellence, that could contribute to strengthen and improve those sacred ties, which at the same time bind the virtuous to the strict performance of their duties here, and the fulfilment of the obligations which they owe to the great hereafter.

It is unnecessary to attempt tracing the sympathies of the human heart in their diversified exercise around the family fireside, or throughout the extended circle of tender relations and devoted friends. It is unnecessary to rend the veil from the kind communion of kindred spirits, and to calculate their vast sum of human worth and enjoyment, by throwing into the account the mutual courtesies, kindnesses, and benefactions by which the wise and the virtuous are ever united together. All these may readily be inferred from the regular, uniform, and consistent denotements of Christian charity and benevolence.

Men may, it is true, in all their familiar and friendly intercourse faithfully perform every duty incumbent upon them in those relations, because character, interest, and *duty* all *combine* to produce and promote that performance, yet, when these motives are *wanting*, the heart may be as cold and cheerless as the mountain snow!

When we bear in mind that temporal death is the dark portal to Eternal Life, we should also remember, as he remembered, that the best commemoration of the beloved departed is that which relates, not merely to this sublunary sphere of action, but to the conscientious discharge of his duties to his Saviour and to his God. While, therefore, we are not to disparage *good* works, high *moral* tendencies, eminent, social or professional accomplishments; which too often perhaps form the subjects of inflated eulogy, we must recollect that in themselves, they are comparatively nothing. Without that supernatural influence arising from an humble and faithful devotion to the Creator, what, alas! is mere *morality*, doing to your neighbor as you would be done by. This is at best but thrifty, frugal honesty. It is nothing for the next world, unless you combine therewith a higher and diviner duty, that of " loving the Almighty with all your mind, with all your heart, and with all your strength." The discharge of our obligations here must be the effluence, or the reflex, of our duties to Heaven, in order that we may secure an Eternal reward. The debt due to Heaven is not satisfied by the fulfilment of mere temporal, or conventional responsibility. The Great Judge does not reward our *acts* alone, he rewards the motive, the conscientious and faithful discharge of our obligations to *him*. That man is *charitable*, who even without the *ability*, has still the desire to relieve the distresses, or pardon, or excuse the faults of others; while *he* may be utterly destitute of charity, *who*, liberally and actually gives or forgives, without a proper and pious sense of Christian obligation. We cannot draw upon the treasury of Heaven to pay the contracts of the mere world. "They are of the earth, earthy," and are entitled to no credit upon the great and final book of Judgment! Nay, they may be even *debited* against us, unless in their motives they represent a celestial influence or agency. In all men do, and say, and think, and suffer, they must recognize, as our departed friend recognized, their liability to the great first cause. In saying this, we must not be supposed to *undervalue* the charms and blandishments of a sincerely virtuous life; but we cannot *overvalue* a pious Christian life. The former belongs often to the *head;*

the latter *must* belong to the *heart* of man; speaking through divine influence, and for divine purposes. *Mere* morality therefore is nothing in itself. Religion, it is true, cannot exist without morality; but what the world calls morality may exist without religion. It is the mere body without the life or spirit. It must be. the *mind* that makes that body *rich.*

In approaching the discharge of my more immediate duty, permit me, now, almost without commentary (for your reflections shall be the commentary), incidentally, to refer to the pure and patriotic and honored ancestry of my present subject.

Jared Ingersoll, the father of our lamented friend, was born in the year seventeen hundred and forty-nine, and died in eighteen hundred and twenty-two. He graduated at Yale College in seventeen hundred and sixty-six, and shortly after went to England, where he entered the Middle Temple, and passed five years in the study of the Law. Shortly after this the Revolution broke out, and he at once attached himself, though the son of a loyalist, to the cause of the Colonies. From London he passed to Paris, where he remained two years; and finally returning to this country, took up his residence in Philadelphia, and occupied at once a prominent position as a lawyer. He became a member of the convention which formed the United States Constitution, presided over by Washington. He was afterwards appointed Attorney General of Pennsylvania—subsequently United States District Attorney—and in eighteen hundred and twelve was nominated as a candidate for the Vice-Presidency of the United States. At the time of his death, which took place in 1822, he was President of the District Court of the City and County of Philadelphia.

His eldest son, Charles Jared Ingersoll, a lawyer, statesman, and author, was born October the third, seventeen hundred and eighty-two: and after having been admitted to practice before he came of age, travelled in Europe, became attached to the American Embassy in France, and made a European tour with Rufus King, Minister of the United States. Returning home in 1805, he entered upon the practice of his profession. In 1812 he was elected to Congress. In 1814 he was again a candidate, but was defeated. In 1815 he was appointed by President Madison, United States District Attorney, an office which he continued to hold until 1829. He was again elected to Congress in 1840–42–44, and in 1847 was nominated as Minister to France by President Polk, but the nomination was not confirmed by the Senate.

Joseph R. Ingersoll was the son of Jared Ingersoll and Elizabeth his wife; both of whom having passed the allotted term of threescore years and ten, were gathered to their fathers. And here, in passing, we owe a just tribute to the unassuming virtues and influences of maternal love, a matter always to be considered, but too often forgotten or undervalued.

It is useless to refer to the glorious proverbial examples of the mother of the Gracchi, or the mother of Shakspeare, or of Sir William Jones, or of Washington; for I maintain that to maternal influence and instruction we often owe more than even to those of the father. The first lessons are the deepest, most lasting, and most available. What is the harvest without seed-time; your culture without the soil; your building without the foundation? Many distinguished fathers have produced obscure sons, a truly wise mother, almost never! Circumstances and casualties may affect or control this principle, but it is still well-founded in nature and experience. Unobtrusive female influences are often lost sight of; yet, in estimating the value of a man's character, it would be, in most cases, safer to inquire, who was his MOTHER, than who was his FATHER. And we cannot help thinking that when the elder Ingersoll wrote to his son at Princeton, as he did, to remember the " HONORS," he might as well have added, remember, also, the precepts and injunctions of your mother. It is obvious, however, that the subject of our present notice enjoyed all the early and appropriate advantages imparted by *both* his parents. But it is not requisite further to unfold the memorials of the ancestry of the subject of this sketch: it is enough to say that it was a good tree, that furnished good and precious fruit; as was amply manifested in the life, character, and death of our lamented friend, to whose career our attention, and our reverential and affectionate sympathies are this night to be devoted.

Joseph R. Ingersoll was born on the fourteenth day of June, seventeen hundred and eighty-six, as the father's record states, "on the rising of the sun." After having read law with his father with great assiduity he was admitted to practice on the second day of June, 1807, and died on the twentieth day of February, eighteen hundred and sixty-eight, in the eighty-second year of his age. Of some men this might be all that the world would desire, or deserve, or expect to know. Not so with the illustrious departed. He is gone, it is true, but his memory should still survive as a bright and lasting example, showing the height to which a life of virtue raises mortal man. His worth and his virtues were commensurate with his years. He was a man of genial alacrity, of systematic and untiring industry, of refined manners, of a frank and urbane spirit, exemplary integrity, and a most signal example of benevolence. As a lawyer he combined all the requirements of his diversified profession. He was thoroughly read in legal science, thoroughly skilled in its practice. Each one of these qualifications contributed to brighten and improve the others, in the reflection of mutual and reciprocal light, and like a glorious constellation, imparted lustre to the entire profession. And in addition to all, he possessed the power of a most persuasive elo-

2

quence, which was never surpassed, if ever equalled, at the American bar.

He was in truth a great orator. The fine arts, polite literature, in short the Graces and the Muses were all tributary to his formation and success. They may all be won by labor, and without labor they will assuredly all be lost. Incessant study loses its fancied severity by being universal and various. Mental exercise and mental enjoyment are perfected by diffusion as well as by concentration, and this remark is peculiarly appropriate to oratory. The mind of the orator should be directed to history, mathematics, metaphysics, poetry, music, painting, and sculpture, in order that he may comprehend that intellectual relation, that secret charm in the liberal professions which, connecting one with another, combines the influence of all. Oratory is distinguished, because it requires, implies, and imparts extensive knowledge. It is a mistake to suppose that accomplishment in speech indicates a want of accomplishment in thought; as, for instance, that a great speaker cannot be a great statesman, a great lawyer, or an eminent divine. Look at Pitt, and silver-tongued Murray, were they not great statesmen? Marshall, Pinkney, Webster, Brougham, Erskine, and Dupin, were among the greatest lawyers of their respective countries; yet their power of speech secured them more fame, fortune, and promotion, than *without* it, all their law learning could have acquired.

The advocate compared with a mere lawyer, is "Hyperion to a Satyr."

After his admission Mr. Ingersoll soon found himself in a large and active practice, and here, although there is no occasion for professional anecdotes, yet you must allow me to introduce one as an early characteristic of Mr. Ingersoll's ambition.

In the year 1810 he was inquired of by Mr. William Lewis, one of the oldest and most distinguished lawyers of the bar, whether he would not like to argue a case in the Supreme Court at Washington. This to an ambitious young man was a tempting intimation, as it was calculated at once to lay the foundation for professional eminence and fortune. He therefore accepted the proffered employment. I think it was the case of Fitzimmons and others against Ogden and others, reported in 7th Cranch. The case was a highly important one, it was the first case on the list of the court, and the term was to commence in three days. Mr. Lewis gave him all the information he could, furnished the notes of his argument, and, full of trepidation and hope, he and his colleague proceeded to Washington. The cause required months of preparation, but as he had entered upon the task, there was no time to retract. The counsel opposed were Richard Stockton and David B. Ogden, who were ready and eager for the conflict. It so happened, however, that Chief Justice Marshall, on his way from Richmond, met with an accident which fractured his collar bone, and

Judge Johnson, of South Carolina, was prevented from attending court by sickness in his family. Of course the court held no session, and the case was postponed for a year; at the expiration of which time our young aspirant for professional fame was abundantly prepared, argued his case with signal ability, and with the entire approval of his learned colleague and the court, and returned to the city, not only decked out in "golden opinions," but bearing in his purse a *golden* fee of one hundred guineas.

Audentes fortuna juvat.

Prior to this he had made several speeches in the Supreme Court of the State of Pennsylvania, that gave an earnest of the rich harvest of professional fame which he was destined by his genius, his talents, and his labors, subsequently to acquire.

In the case of Pullen *vs.* Salter, in which he was associated with Mr. Binney, for the plaintiff, and which was founded upon a grievous assault committed by the defendant upon a helpless child, he not only succeeded in convicting the defendant in a criminal court, but he recovered, upon a civil action, a large verdict, the amount of which was vested in him as trustee for the benefit of the child, and finally paid over by him with its accumulated interest, upon the arrival of his client at maturity.

The first case wherein I personally encountered him at the bar was in the year 1818. The case of the commonwealth against Alderman Binns, which in most of its features resembled that last spoken of. I

was counsel for the commonwealth, and Mr. Ingersoll represented the defendant. It was a case of
great excitement, and occupied several days in its
trial. Being, as has been said, my *first* case, before
commencing my speech, I turned to Mr. Ingersoll,
although my antagonist, and said, "This is a terrific
ordeal, very much like facing a full mouthed-battery."
"Yes," was the reply, "it is truly a great day for you,
as you may probably date your *rise* or *ruin* from it."

"I," he continued, "had a similar case very early
in my practice, in which I happened to succeed, and
I have felt the influence of it upon my professional
career ever since." This remark was not very en-
couraging to me at the time, but no doubt it proved
very salutary.

For thirty years the history of his life was the
history of the bar. He was the cynosure of all eyes,
the observed of all observers. Other countries and
other states may boast of their distinguished jurists
and advocates, but the bar of Pennsylvania, in its
palmy days, defies all rivalry or competition. And
when he withdrew from the bar, together with Horace
Binney, John B. Wallace, Charles Chauncey, John
Seargeant, and Dallas, a gap was left in its professional history that, perhaps, during *our* time at least,
will never be filled up. *They* have, however, thrown
a halo of glory over their successors, which should be
valued and guarded as a rich inheritance, and which,
if not increased, should at least be preserved and
bequeathed to those who follow us.

Mr. Ingersoll sometimes took full notes of his forensic speeches, which were beautifully and logically
arranged, and with the greatest care. Not that it was
necessary to him, but in some instances he deemed
it essential to the subject, though he rarely referred
to his manuscript; and it could scarcely be perceived
that it was in any way relied upon.

He spoke equally well upon all occasions. His
language was pure, ornate, and most graphic, and
his manner was a study for a forensic speaker. He
was not what you would call a keen or subtle lawyer,
who may have a sharp *wedge*, but no *maul* to drive
it. The jury, therefore, was always ready to believe
what he said, from his general candor and honesty,
and it is much to be doubted whether he ever lost a
cause, which he ought to have gained.

He had great delicacy and purity of conversation.
He had all the refinements of a woman, with the
energy of a man. He was a most distinguished
colloquist. His mind was not only a library of useful
knowledge, but, it was a *circulating* library; not re-
served and locked up for the purpose of occasional
display, but free and bountiful as the atmosphere by
which he was surrounded.

It is a difficult thing to compress the scenes and
services of an active life of fourscore years, within
the narrow limits of a single hour. But the difficulty
is diminished, upon the present occasion, in the belief
that I am addressing those who are familiar with the
bright pages, of which I represent merely the index.

Of the career of some men it might be said, they were born, they lived, and they died ; but not so of one the span of whose life embraced the diversified practical exercise of all the social, moral, professional, and Christian duties.

Although we admit the mind is the standard of the man, as the jewel is the treasure of the casket, we may be permitted, if not expected to present a scanty sketch at least of the *exterior* of one, whose mental qualities were so beautiful, so various, and so harmonious.

In person, Mr. Ingersoll was somewhat above the medium height, of light complexion, bright blue eyes, auburn hair, small features, and of a slender, lithe, and active frame. In his dress he was always scrupulously neat. In his *address* he was familiar and cheerful to all, without being contaminated by any. He possessed a placid temper. I have tried cases with him and against him, that, from their excitement and peril, not only stirred men's blood, but made the hair stand on end, and the whole community look aghast! and yet I never knew him to lose his equanimity or composure for a single moment. In the trials of what were called the church riots, Orange riots, and Kensington riots, which lasted for months, and I might almost say for years, during which your streets flowed with blood ; and outrage, disorder, and murder pervaded large portions of this community, he pursued his calm and steady course, and smiled as serenely as the sun amidst an elemental war!

He manifested no signs of labor, was systematic in the performance of all his various duties, and characterized by the strictest sense of honor and propriety in his entire intercourse with the court, the bar, and the country. But that was not all : he was a man of exemplary piety, without the least Pharisaical pretension. In short, he combined the Lawyer with the unsophisticated Christian, and in the language of one who never fails,

> " So *far behind* his worth,
> Come all the praises that we now bestow :
> He was complete, in feature and in mind,
> With all good grace, to grace a GENTLEMAN."

Even in his afflictions, although he felt deeply, he never evinced a repining spirit. He was deprived of the beloved partner of his bosom, two sons, and a daughter ; and although bending beneath those grievous blows, his spirit was never broken, but looked with a sublime eye upon these dispensations and decrees of an all-wise Judge. Cut loose, however, from those tender and endearing domestic attachments, he finally withdrew from the toils of the bar, and devoted his attention to the charms of a refined literature, and to the inestimable and inexhaustible treasures of Holy Writ, the Great Book of Eternal Life! So he lived, and so at length he died, in the humble hope, through Redeeming love, of being gathered to the companionship of the just made perfect.

Having thus furnished a hasty outline of the portrait of our departed friend, it is with mingled pain and pleasure that we now turn to some of the more particular details and coloring of the picture.

He had a fine poetical taste, a high appreciation of the charms of poetry, and ancient and modern literature. Although he *wrote* but little himself, he *read* much, and thereby relieved while he improved his professional labor. There was a classic beauty in his mind, of which of course his language largely partook. He was never overbearing, and not to be overborne. He was a most generous, genial, and confiding friend.

All orders and departments of learning reciprocally borrow and reflect light, and, in their united influence, constitute the truly accomplished man. Each and all *require* labor, while they relieve, sweeten, and *reward* labor. You may have ever so rich a quarry, but without the chisel and the mallet the glorious statues will sleep there forever.

Industry is not natural to man, it may become habitual, or it may be stimulated by necessity, or a desire of gain ; but with *him*, it was apparently a matter at once of duty and delight; and yet his efforts were so regulated and systematized as to afford him abundant opportunity for all the social enjoyments and virtues and happiness of life : so that he might be said to be a devout student, and a most accomplished gentleman, at the same time. He was not a demonstrative man; it was not in his nature to be vain or obtrusive. He rarely talked of himself, or his profession, or his professional brethren. He had no jealousies, for his position was above them. He had no enemies, except among those who were enemies to virtue. He was a man of high and excitable spirit, and of undoubted courage; but those qualities were so tempered by a most generous and charitable heart, and by a sense of self-respect, that they were rarely, if indeed ever, unnecessarily displayed. He was, as I have said, a warm, cherished, and faithful friend, a charitable and most generous benefactor, a tender and devoted relative, an unshaken patriot, and an honest man. To say this and *all* this is to say no more than the experience of all who knew *him*, and now hear *me*, will abundantly confirm. Alas! he is gone, and the place that knew him shall know him no more! But he has left to survivors the cherished memory of his virtues to be embalmed, and his spotless example to be imitated.

Will my kind friends allow me here to recall what has been omitted in its proper place, but which is still deemed pertinent to the objects of this occasion?

In the course of these remarks I have incidentally referred to the father and his distinguished sons—a glorious triumvirate, all figuring at the same time! History, we may add, scarcely supplies an example of such brilliant professional powers, exhibited in the same immediate family. Nothing could be more impressive than to behold them either as colleagues, or antagonists in some exciting and important cause—especially in cases wherein they were professionally *opposed*, and when the conflict was beautifully tempered by parental regard and filial or fraternal affection; so that while dutifully struggling for success, their respective hopes of triumph were mingled with grateful sympathies for their opponents. No name, we may add, has ever shed a more lasting forensic lustre upon the annals of the Pennsylvania bar than that of INGERSOLL!

To resume my imperfect sketch. Mr. Ingersoll was a graduate of Princeton in the year 1801, and received the first honors of his class, consisting of Southard, and Frelinghuysen, and others of like distinction—men who magnified their country and themselves! Having studied with his father, he was admitted to the practice of law on the 2d of June, 1807. He united literary with professional labors. He delivered discourses in the various Universities of the nation from Maine to Mexico. Those, and his political and philanthropic discourses, have been published and are extensively known, so as to render all special notice upon this occasion unnecessary if not superfluous. We may be excused in saying, however, that he virtually contributed to give sight to the *blind*, hearing to the *deaf*, speech to the *dumb*, while he also practically and largely promoted the dissemination of literature and science and philanthropy throughout the entire community.

The degrees of "LL. D." and D. C. L. have been repeatedly and deservedly conferred upon him by the highest literary and scientific institutions in our land. Honorable public employments have been enjoyed by him. He was a member of the Board of Trustees of the University of Pennsylvania; a delegate to the diocesan and general conventions of the Protestant Episcopal Church; President of the Academy of Fine Arts; President of Select Council; member of the Philosophical Society; President of the Colonization Society, and President of the Historical Society.

He was elected to Congress in 1836 and 1837, and then, having declined a *re-election*, he was afterwards elected in 1842; again in 1847, and has since been continued, by increasing majorities. He was the author of the minority report of the Committee of "Ways and Means" of this same Congress against the *assumption of State debts*, and an issue of two hundred millions of United States bonds for distribution among the States. He opposed the *repeal of the tariff* of 1842 (in the 28th Congress), and drew an elaborate report against that repeal on behalf of the minority of the committee. He spoke against the *annexation of Texas*. In the session of 1849, the *sub-treasury law* was also opposed by him. On the Oregon question he delivered an earnest and masterly speech *against the fifty-four-forty* doctrine, and in favor of an amicable adjustment of the dangerous controversy therein involved. In the 30th Congress he became Chairman of the Judiciary Committee, in the duties of which high station he manifested the most untiring industry and distinguished ability.

In the year 1852 he was appointed, by President Fillmore, Minister to England, where he remained and exercised his functions with great distinction until the expiration of Mr. Fillmore's term of office, when he returned to Philadelphia and retired to private life.

Allow me again to say, Mr. Ingersoll was a ripe and an accomplished lawyer, possessed of all the learning that the duties of his profession demanded. It was truly said of Shakspeare, the brightest genius of the world, that if he had been more deeply learned it might have impaired and cramped his genius, and he would have thought or written less or worse. As of Milton it has been observed, that if he had spared a little learning "Paradise Lost" would have been much improved. So it may be truly said of our subject, that if he had studied more, or *could have* studied more, his efficiency and triumphant success, in the vast variety of his practice, would in all human probability have been impaired. He was indefatigably industrious. His whole disposable time was constantly employed, not upon any exclusive subject, but upon cases of the most diversified and complicated character. His original foundations in the law were laid broad and deep and strong, and fully sustained during half a century, the beautiful superstructure and embellishments which his taste, his fancy, and his talents thereon erected.

He was never known to be taken by surprise, or to appeal for indulgence; nor, what is more, I never knew him to refuse indulgence to others, when reasonably requested.

He faithfully represented his client, and *did* what he thought his client *ought* to do. He never forgot his moral or social obligations in the discharge of his professional duties. He always bore in mind that an advocate should be a gentleman, that a true gentleman should be a Christian, one of the Almighty's NOBLEMEN. He neither buried nor perverted the talent with which he had been intrusted by his divine Master, but applied it to the great purposes of his Creator, in clothing the naked, feeding the hungry, sustaining the feeble, opening the eyes of the blind, and proving a friend and a father to the poor, the outcast, and the wretched. The result was, the accumulation of an ample fortune, and without a spot, or blur, or blemish upon his personal or professional fame.

We are aware that it has been said, that with all these accomplishments, he was not a very profound lawyer. So it was said of Lord Bacon, to whom Sir Thomas Fleming was preferred to the chief justiceship of the King's Bench, simply because, says Lord Campbell, "*he* was a *mere* lawyer, and did not mortify the vanity of the witty, nor alarm the jealousy of the ambitious."

So also it was charged against Lord Mansfield, by the envious and vulgar of his time, who are always eager to pull down those who soar above them, and insist that if a man is celebrated for elegant accomplishments he can have no law, and if he is distinguished as a deep lawyer, he can have no elegant accomplishments.

Again, upon the creation of Lord Brougham to the Lord Chancellorship of Great Britain, Sir Edward Sugden, who was his competitor, observed: "What a pity it is that the Lord Chancellor knows nothing of Equity." Upon this being communicated to Brougham, he pithily remarked: "It is a much greater pity that Sir Edward should know nothing else!"

The very variety and activity of professional employment may distract the best mind, and prevent that concentration of thought essential to a laborious and devoted investigation. Men like Sir Fletcher Norton, and Sargeant Maynard, and Chief Justice Holt, may prefer the study of year-books, or the Natura-brevium, or Fearne on Remainders, or the Statutes at Large,—they were great *lawyers*, but certainly not great *men!*

But *he* was not only, as has been said, a great lawyer and thorough advocate, but he was a great man, considered in all the qualifications and combinations of his character, moral, intellectual, social, and religious. To borrow a figure from a powerful speech of his in Congress, he maintained a position "like that which in architecture is said to enhance the magnificence of a Grecian temple, when placed, as it ought to be, on elevated ground, and gaining by distance and unobstructed prospect, at once in grandeur and distinctness for the view it stands unmated and alone!" There may have been more profound lawyers, but none superior to him in eloquence, or in what may be called the aptitudes of his profession, and few equal to him in those graces of character, which, we are told, make ambition a virtue. A great lawyer is not necessarily, we repeat, a great man. Lord Coke was a great lawyer, but a little man ; and if parts allure you, see how Bacon shined, "the wisest, brightest, meanest of mankind." Ingersoll may have been second in some accomplishments to those who were greatest, but those very men were second to him in the diversity, generality, efficiency and purity of his knowledge.

In addition to all these various responsibilities and public duties, he had confided to him the instruction of more students than any other member of the bar in this city ever had. And it may be justly said that they were as well trained, and reflected as much credit upon the preceptor and the profession, as any students from any other quarters. It might be deemed invidious to name them, but some have filled high judicial position, and *all* have contributed largely to the integrity and distinction of the Philadelphia bar.

The course of reading prescribed in his office was thorough. Laying the groundwork in the study of natural, political, and international law, and the popular and elegant commentary of Sir Wm. Blackstone, he led them to the fundamental Doctrines of Tenures and Estates, which were followed by the Standard Treatises, of Preston, Fearne, Powell, and Sugden. Knowing well that without regular and periodical, and thorough digestion, of what had been read, the student would need that stimulus and encouragement so necessary to excite and keep alive an interest in his studies, he subjected them to regular and systematic monthly examinations of the course of studies, explaining what was obscure, and impressing upon them what was most important and essential.

Now, it is not so remarkable that Mr. Ingersoll should have accomplished so much, as that he should invariably accomplish it so well. Without the most rigid method, punctuality, and perseverance, no such results could possibly have been produced. The instructor, therefore, might well have been proud of his pupils, and the pupils (many of whom are still distinguished ornaments of the bar), it is certain, have ever held the name of their master in grateful, affectionate, and reverential remembrance.

He was blessed, as has been said, with two sons and a daughter. The sons died in early infancy. In the year eighteen hundred and thirty-three he lost his affectionate wife, with whom he had lived nearly a quarter of a century. She was the daughter of

Alexander Wilcox, formerly an eminent member of
the ancient Philadelphia bar; a woman of great
personal attractions, an amiable temper, and most
refined and accomplished manners.

He was now left with but one child, a daughter—
a delicate, fragile, and beautiful girl, the last sur-
viving pledge of mutual affection, who, after having
just reached the prime of life, was suddenly torn by
remorseless death, from the arms of her devoted
father.

> Sweet rose, fair flower, untimely pluck'd, soon faded,
> Plucked in the bud and faded in the spring.

Thus bereft, what had he in this world to live for?
It has been poetically, though truly said, that the
crowning sorrow of all earthly sorrows, is the
memory of past joys, past, never to return!

Thus afflicted, after having been surrounded by all
the embellishments and attractions of the world, what
remained, alas! of comfort and consolation, what lessons of human philosophy could impart solace to the
wounds and sufferings of his heart. For agonies like
these there was "no balm in Gilead, no physician
there!" In the consciousness of destitution of all
worldly aid, all temporal hope, his thoughts were
turned to Heaven, in the Christian assurance that
God, and God *only*, can heal the wounds that he in-
flicts! If we cannot, in the hour of affliction, gain
support from religion, it is not that religion cannot
furnish it; but because we want faith in its efficacy.

All that the earth could confer, he had enjoyed; all the loss he could suffer, he had sustained; and should "we receive good at the hands of the Lord and not evil!"

> Then let us thank the Eternal Power, convinced
> That Heaven but tries our virtue by affliction;
> That oft the cloud that wraps the present hour,
> Serves but to *brighten* all our future days.

As a son, a husband, a father, and a brother, he had discharged and embellished the full measure of his duties; and deprived by Almighty wisdom of all those tender endearments and blessings, he clothed himself with humble resignation, and awaited in Christian hope the inevitable doom! All this world's suffering, like this world's glory, leads but to the grave, the place appointed for all living :—

> "Death is the crown or crucifix of fame."

I knew him, perhaps, better than any other living man; and no one could value him more highly, or deplore his loss more deeply.

His morals were of the highest order; they were the morals of religion, as spoken of in the outset of this discourse; they pointed directly to heaven; the purity of his life was in accordance with his sublime responsibilities to a higher power. No man ever heard him express a sentiment inconsistent with his Christian calling or profession; in the observance of which duties his fidelity was so exemplary. The warmth of his heart, like the sun, irradiated the whole horizon of his life, while his innate modesty and piety never let his left hand know what his right hand did.

If he were not so remarkable as some men, it was because there was so beautiful a harmony in his talents and his virtues; so free from the dark shadows that are sometimes attendant upon greatness, as to astonish and attract us less, in contemplating the lights of the portrait.

But why should we longer linger upon those worldly triumphs and distinctions? What are they all! He is GONE, and the place that knew him shall know him no more. And now look at the *grave*, and tell me what they all come to! How much do they partake of *this* world, and how *little* of the next? They are grateful to the sense of those who loved him, but they are fleeting and illusory! A few short years shall bury the remembrance of the brightest and the best in this world's annals. The only record that shall endure is the imperishable Record of Heaven! While therefore we may be allowed to commemorate the earthly career of men, and thus sooth the feelings of sorrowful and sympathizing relatives and friends, we should bear always in mind that the crowning glory is the GREAT HEREAFTER!

Too much familiarity with the public, in an old man, has been said to be an indignity to human nature, and a neglect of divine nature. Of age the glory is the wish to die. Be this as it may, towards the close of his life, he comparatively withdrew from the activity and bustle of this world, and restricted his intercourse, for the most part, to a limited circle of his endearing relatives and friends.

He passed the fourscore years of his life without most of its ordinary physical infirmities (though he encountered, as we have said, changing and afflicting vicissitudes); and finally relinquished the fleeting attractions of this sublunary sphere for the immarcescible triumphs of Eternal Life! Well indeed might he, and with still *greater* faith, have exclaimed with his great Roman exemplar and prototype, "I am far from regretting my temporal life, as I have the satisfaction to think that I have lived in such a manner as not to have lived in vain; I consider this world as a place which nature never designed for my permanent abode: and I look upon my departure, not as being driven from my habitation, but as leaving my Inn. Oh! glorious day, when I retire from the toils and scenes of this world, to associate with the divine assemblage of departed spirits!"

Alas, he is gone! but has left us the cherished memory of his virtues to be embalmed, and the benefit of his bright example to be imitated; while then we mourn our loss, let us not forget that our loss is his immortal gain; let us endeavor to emulate his virtues, and thus secure to ourselves, through the merits of Redeeming Love, Heaven's promised blessings to the just made perfect.

'Tis nothing thus to die, but to prepare !
To free our earthborn thoughts from their deep root ;
To fix our faith, not on the passing world,
Those fleeting pageants of terrestrial joy,

That sicken, languish, rot in our embrace,
But on the world to come, which never fades,
Passes nor changes, brighter than day dawn ;
More lasting than the stars, where sits enthroned
The Great Jehovah ! Universal Lord !

The orator closed amid applause.

Colonel J. Ross Snowden then said :—

Mr. President: I will detain you and the audience but a few moments. A Society whose chief
object is to collect and preserve historical matter per-
taining to our State and nation, is in the proper discharge of its functions, when it takes official notice of
citizens who have rendered distinguished services to
their country. The biography of such citizens serves
to make up the materials of history. But we have,
in the case of Mr. Ingersoll, an additional motive. He
was, at the time of his decease, and for several years
preceding that event, the President of our Society.

Advancing years, with its physical infirmities, in
the latter period of his life, prevented him from regu-
larly occupying the President's chair. And I may
say here that the location of the Society's rooms, in
the third story of a high building—(the Athenæum)
—served to prevent his attendance, and that of many
other honored members—an inconvenience which will
continue to operate against the interests and usefulness of the Society until a more suitable and secure
building, in an appropriate location, is obtained.

Nevertheless, Mr. Ingersoll took a deep interest in the proceedings and operations of the Society, and occasionally attended its meetings. Moreover, he contributed with liberality to its funds.

Mr. Ingersoll possessed all the peculiarities which make up the character of an eminent, useful, and good citizen. He was distinguished for wisdom and sound learning, and eminent for his probity and high sense of the proprieties and duties of life.

It is to lives and characters like his, that Philadelphia is indebted for her high position as a seat of learning, of science, and of literature; which, together with her educated merchants, artists, and manufacturers, and men of the learned professions, make her the metropolis of a great State, and a chief city of a grand country.

In bringing forward to a conspicuous view the life and character of such citizens as Joseph Reed Ingersoll, we not only give honor where honor is due, but we render some service to our country, by setting before the people proper subjects for their example and imitation.

It is not my purpose, however, to enlarge upon this interesting theme, nor to add anything to what has been so well and appropriately said by the eloquent orator who has addressed us this evening. But as a further testimonial of our regard for the memory of our late President, I offer the following resolutions :—

Resolved, That the exercises of this evening, arranged and carried into effect by the Historical Society of Pennsylvania, are intended to express its high admiration of the character, public services, and private virtues of its late distinguished and venerable President, Mr. Ingersoll, and that the members of the Society will hold his memory in the highest respect and regard.

Resolved, That the thanks of the Society, and of this audience, be presented to David Paul Brown, Esq., for his eloquent and appropriate eulogium on the life and character of Mr. Ingersoll, and that he be requested to furnish a copy of it, to be placed among the archives of the Society.

Resolved, That the eulogium delivered by Mr. Brown, together with the proceedings of this meeting, be published under the direction of the appropriate committee of the Society.

The resolutions were seconded by H. G. Jones, Esq., and unanimously adopted. The audience then retired.

www.ingramcontent.com/pod-product-compliance
Lightning Source LLC
Chambersburg PA
CBHW061237260626
47172CB00003B/901